WOODROW AT SEA

Wallace Edwards

pajamapress

First published in Canada in 2017
First published in the United States in 2018
Text and illustration copyright © 2017 Wallace Edwards
This edition copyright © 2017 Pajama Press Inc.
This is a first edition.

10 9 8 7 6 5 4 3 2 1

www.pajamapress.ca   info@pajamapress.ca

Canada Council   Conseil des arts
for the Arts   du Canada

ONTARIO ARTS COUNCIL
CONSEIL DES ARTS DE L'ONTARIO
an Ontario government agency
un organisme du gouvernement de l'Ontario

Canadä

The publisher gratefully acknowledges the support of the Canada Council for the Arts and the Ontario Arts Council for its publishing program. We acknowledge the financial support of the Government of Canada through the Canada Book Fund (CBF) for our publishing activities.

Library and Archives Canada Cataloguing in Publication

Edwards, Wallace, author, illustrator
      Woodrow at sea / Wallace Edwards. -- First edition.
ISBN 978-1-77278-029-1 (hardcover)
      1. Stories without words. I. Title.
PS8559.D88W66 2017   jC813'.6   C2017-904449-4

Publisher Cataloging-in-Publication Data (U.S.)

Names: Edwards, Wallace, author, illustrator.
Title: Woodrow at Sea / Wallace Edwards.
Description: Toronto, Ontario Canada : Pajama Press, 2017. | Summary: "In this wordless picture book, Woodrow the elephant rows off to find adventure and discovers a mouse marooned at sea. As the two go through many adventures and rescue each other from dangers, they discover that the best thing to find on a journey is a true friend"— Provided by publisher.
Identifiers: ISBN 978-1-77278-029-1 (hardcover)
Subjects: LCSH: Elephants – Juvenile fiction. | Mice – Juvenile fiction. | Friendship – Juvenile fiction. | Stories without words. | BISAC: JUVENILE FICTION / Animals / Elephants. | JUVENILE FICTION / Social Themes / Friendship.
Classification: LCC PZ7.E383Wo |DDC [E] – dc23

Cover and book design—Rebecca Bender

Manufactured by Qualibre Inc/Printplus
Printed in China

Pajama Press Inc.
181 Carlaw Ave. Suite 207 Toronto, Ontario Canada, M4M 2S1

Distributed in Canada by UTP Distribution
5201 Dufferin Street Toronto, Ontario Canada, M3H 5T8

Distributed in the U.S. by Ingram Publisher Services
1 Ingram Blvd. La Vergne, TN 37086, USA

Original art created
with watercolor and ink

To Katie, my love

And to Gordon, George, Leonie, Chase, Miles, Genevieve, Abigail, Sage, and Caitlin

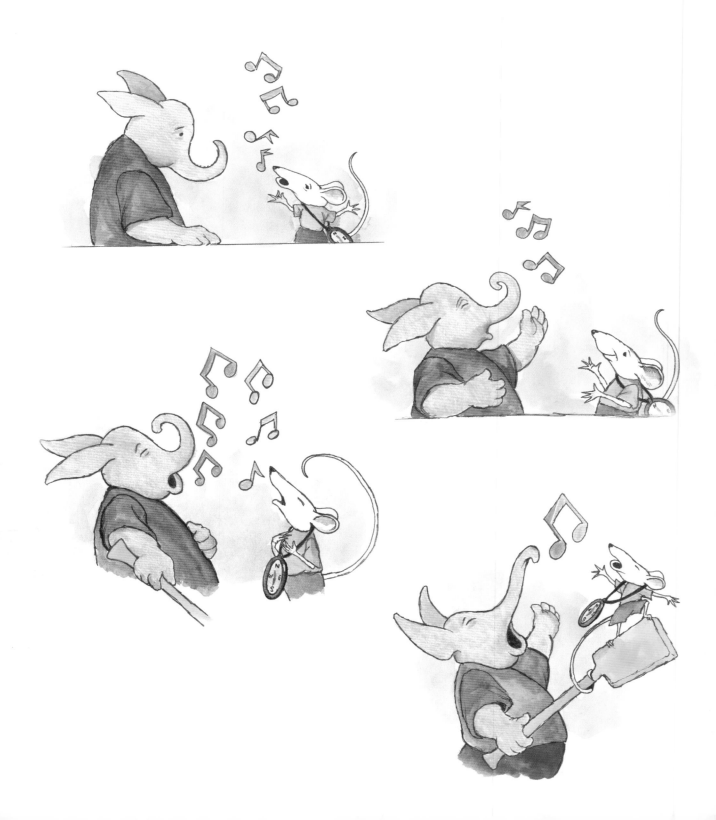

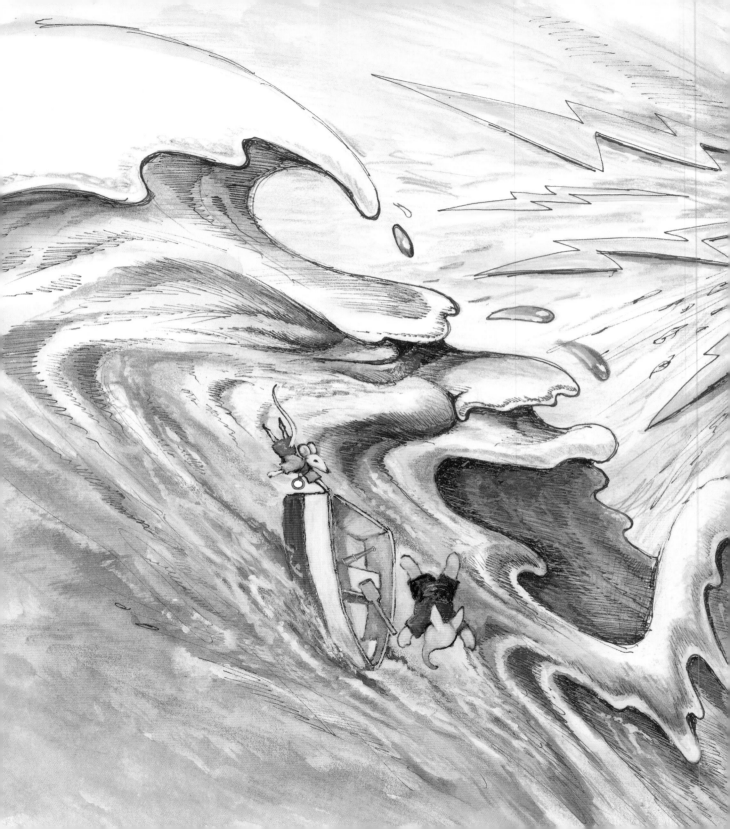

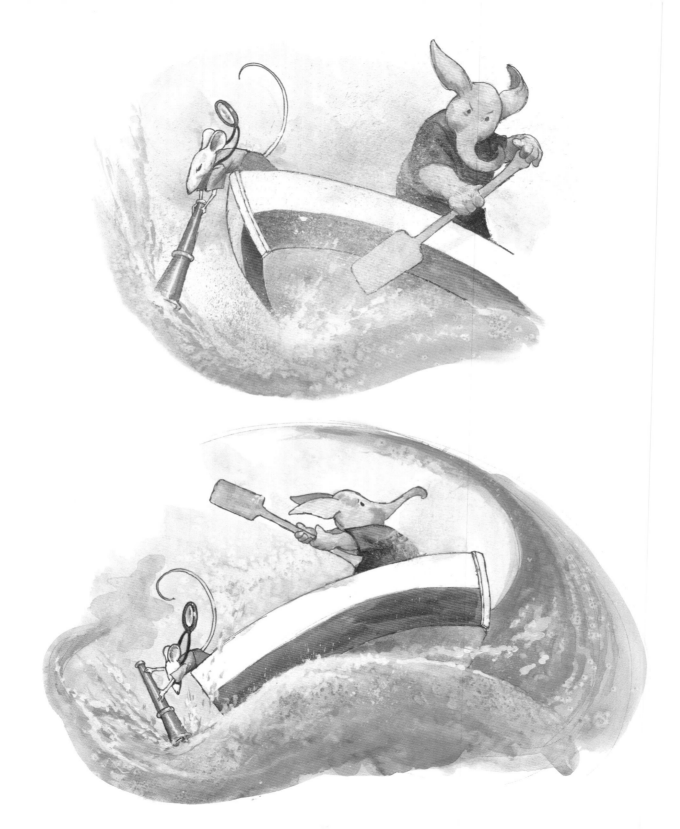

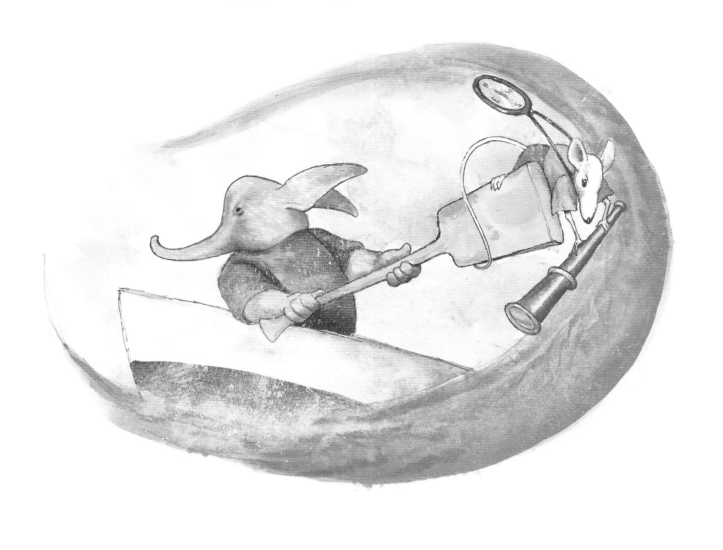

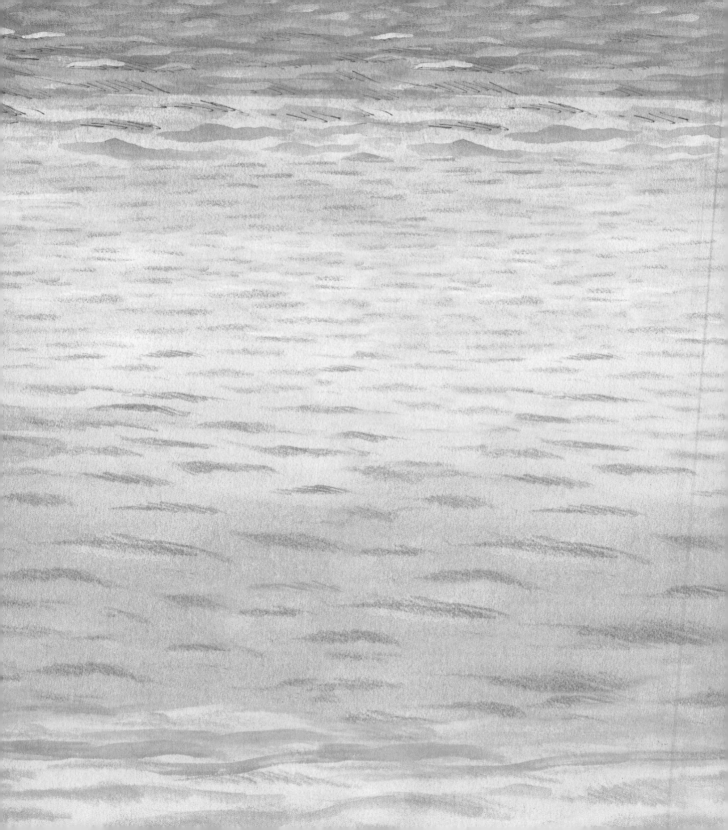